TEEN MENTAL HEALTH

online
bullying

Peter Ryan

ROSEN
PUBLISHING

Published in 2012 by The Rosen Publishing Group, Inc.
29 East 21st Street, New York, NY 10010

First Edition

Library of Congress Cataloging-in-Publication Data

Ryan, Peter.
Online bullying / Peter Ryan.—1st ed.
    p. cm.—(Teen mental health)
Includes bibliographical references and index.
ISBN 978-1-4488-4588-0 (library binding)
1. Cyberbullying—Juvenile literature. I. Title.
HV6773.15.C92R93 2010
302.3—dc22

2011000541

Manufactured in the United States of America

CPSIA Compliance Information: Batch #S11YA: For further information, contact Rosen Publishing, New York, New York, at 1-800-237-9932.

contents

chapter one   The Nature of Bullying   **4**

chapter two   Online Bullying and
the Law   **16**

chapter three   Identifying Online Bullying   **22**

chapter four   How to Prevent Online
Bullying   **29**

chapter five   Documenting Online
Bullying   **34**

glossary   **39**

for more information   **41**

for further reading   **45**

index   **47**

chapter one

The Nature of Bullying

Have you ever been bullied? How did you feel afterward? You've probably been the victim of a bully, been a bully, or seen someone else be bullied. Bullying is very common and often goes unnoticed, and the damage it causes often goes untreated.

Many people assume that bullies and victims only behave one way. The truth is that many bullies are often victims of bullying, and many victims of bullying often become bullies themselves. Researchers have found that there are bullies, victims, bully-victims, and bystanders.

Bully-victims both bully others and are victims of bullying. Bystanders are usually people who don't bully others and aren't victims, but they are witnesses of bullying and their lack of intervention is a contributing part of the bullying cycle.

What may surprise most people is that the outcome of bullying leaves both the victim and the bully feeling awful after an incident of bullying. Researchers have learned that many bullies use bullying because they lack some basic and important social skills. Researchers have also found that bullies who do not receive intervention are more likely to have long-term problems with school, the law, and interpersonal relationships. Bullies suffer from their own behavior.

Many bullies are victims of bullying outside of school, at home, from parents, or from siblings. Because they are bullied, they develop low self-esteem and negative feelings, which they try to cope with by bullying others. This is called the cycle of bullying. This kind of bully who is also a victim of bullying is called a bully-victim.

Just like normal bullying, online bullying, or "cyberbullying," is used to cause intentional harm or disturbance. However, the tools used to bully are things like cell phones and the Internet. Cyberbullying can be both direct and indirect and can be both verbal and relational.

The biggest difference between regular bullying and online bullying is that the bullies are not limited to attacking victims in person: bullies can be complete strangers from far away, and the attacks can be very harmful to the victim. Online bullies also have a much larger pool of victims and a much larger audience. Victims are no longer

Mobile devices make communicating easy, but they also make online bullying easy, too.

able to escape bullying in the safety of their own home. The acts of online bullies are very difficult to undo on the Internet, making their actions and the consequences permanently visible.

Cyberbullying has many forms including e-mail, texting, polling, video posting, Web sites, and, most damaging, sexting—sexting can lead to criminal charges that can label cyberbullies sexual offenders for life. Cyberbullies have many ways that they can cause harm to their victims, and because of the anonymity of the Internet, it makes finding the bully very difficult.

In today's world of electronic communication, bullying has evolved. Bullies can get to their victims no matter where they are, including in their homes. This is very difficult for victims of bullying because they no longer have a safe place to escape from their bullies.

Classifications of Bullying

Bullies use both direct and indirect methods to do their damage. Direct methods can be both physical and verbal bullying; indirect bullying is usually referred to as relational. Direct bullying is when a bully does or says something to the intended victim. Indirect bullying occurs when the bully does something that affects the victim without directly interfering with the victim.

Physical bullying is meant to disturb, hurt, scare, threaten, intimidate, or upset others physically. Bullies use physical attacks when they think victims won't do anything back or when they think victims are not strong enough to stand up for themselves. Physical bullying is most commonly performed by boys, but it can also be done by girls. Victims of physical bullying are usually smaller or weaker than their bully, and the effects of the bullying can leave both physical and emotional scars.

Verbal bullying is using words to inflict harm. Unlike physical bullying, there is no evidence of violence—just the emotional pain and suffering inside the mind of the victim. Verbal bullying usually takes the form of name-calling, taunting, interrupting, teasing, joking or threatening, intimidating, and humiliating. Victims of verbal bullies are often shy, have low self-confidence, and are chosen because they

Bullies target both boys and girls. Despite their gender, bullying victims are equally affected by the abuse.

don't have friends to defend them. Verbal bullying is done by both boys and girls.

Relational bullying is a kind of bullying that creates social discomfort for victims. This kind of bullying affects victims' social status and is most commonly employed by girls, but is used by boys as well. Typically this kind of bullying is used to hurt victims by exposing them to a large audience for embarrassment, humiliation, or isolation. Relational bullying is thought of as indirect bullying because the bully can spread lies about the victim to other people, which then negatively affects the victim. Spreading rumors to ruin someone's reputation is an example of indirect, relational bullying.

Cyberbullying Suicide ("Bullycide"): The Story of Tyler Clementi

Tyler Clementi was a freshman at Rutgers University in New Jersey and a very gifted and talented musician with a

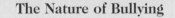

bright future. He was the victim of very harsh bullying episodes. Clementi's roommate and a hallmate secretly recorded Clementi having a sexual encounter with another male student and then streamed the video to other students. On September 22, 2010, Clementi committed suicide.

Clementi initially tried to do the right thing by going to his resident adviser to reveal the incident, requesting that he be assigned to a different room or a different roommate. Shortly after reporting the first incident, Clementi's roommate broadcast a second video of a sexual encounter between Clementi and a male student. A short while after the second video was broadcast, Clementi took his own life by jumping off the George Washington Bridge into the Hudson River.

Clementi's case is not uncommon. Many LGBT (lesbian, gay, bisexual and transgendered) youth face bullying and abuse every day. Because they are different, they are much

Tyler Clementi committed suicide on September 22, 2010, after his sexual encounter with another man in his Rutgers dorm room was secretly videotaped and posted online.

9

more frequently picked on than others, and it is only recently that their suffering has been recognized. There are many support groups now working to help bullied LGBT youth cope with their emotions and help spread awareness about support networks for them.

Clementi's bullies were both arrested and now face third-degree charges of recording a person in a sexual encounter without their consent and possibly second-degree charges related to hate-based crimes and dissemination of the video. These are serious charges, and both of the perpetrators face the prospect of being expelled from Rutgers and serving time in prison.

The Impact of Bullying

Bullying can have a long-lasting, painful impact on both the bully and the victim. Some victims' feelings of pain and hurt are so great that they can lead to violence and suicide. Victims of bullying often have difficulty with interpersonal relationships and can suffer from long-term problems with self-confidence and other emotional disorders.

Bullies themselves can develop long-term problems from their bullying behavior. Although it may not seem possible, bullies often develop emotional and behavioral problems similar to those of the victims of bullying. Researchers have found that there is some connection between bullying and having problems finishing school.

The impact of the cycle of bullying is harmful and long-lasting. It can be broken if teachers, parents, and counselors are brought in to intervene. Bullies can be taught to treat others with respect and develop social skills to have normal relationships. Victims can be taught to develop stronger self-confidence and learn how to prevent situations from becoming bully situations.

Where Does Cyberbullying Happen?

Cyberbullying can happen on social networks like Facebook. There have been many cases where the bully creates a fake social network account about, or even pretending to be, the victim. Social

The emotional pain a bullying victim feels can last much longer than any physical scrape or bruise. Attacking a person emotionally has a real impact.

networks are always on the lookout for bullying and abusive behavior, and most social networks have the right to cancel the account of anyone found to abuse the rules of conduct.

Cell phone bullying is also a major problem. Text wars, a kind of bullying in which a bully will enlist others to help send hundreds of text messages to the victim, can be very intimidating and can be very costly the parents of the victim who may have to pay for the incoming texts. Another cell phone issue is "sexting," or sending sexually explicit photographs or text via SMS texting.

Web sites are often used by bullies to distribute hurtful images or pictures. Some bullies have been found to have created entire Web sites for the sole purpose of hurting a single person. These Web sites are accessible by lots of people, and bullies will spread awareness of the Web site to the victim's classmates and peers in order to increase the impact of the bullying.

Video game console networks like Xbox Live and PlayStation allow users to chat with others both in and out of the game, giving bullies the opportunity to victimize. Other games like *World of Warcraft* are also places where cyberbullying frequently occurs. The bullies can both taunt the victim and disrupt the game, a doubly painful experience because video games are one of the few places that many young people can find some relaxation and private time away from their normal school lives.

YouTube has become a hotbed of online bullying because it is very easy to use, and it has an enormous audience. Publicly sharing videos that may humiliate or embarrass others is very common. Happy slapping, posting videos of real-life physical bullying and abuse, is very common. Sharing videos that the victim thought would be private is also very common.

According to *School Library Journal*, researchers have found that cyberbullying happens frequently and many victims don't report the bullying to teachers or parents. The journal states that "72 percent of teens who are frequent Internet users say they've been the victim of online bullying at least once during the past year, with 90 percent of them saying they don't tell their parents about the online incidents, mainly because they feel the need to deal with the problem on their own and are fearful of parental restrictions on Internet use."

Other research has found that "about half (49.5%) of students indicated they had been bullied online and 33.7% indicated they had bullied others online," according to the *American Journal of Orthopsychiatry*. This research is important because it shows how common it is for bullying to occur and not be reported.

Isolation from groups due to bullying can be very harmful. Young people rely on friends for a sense of well-being.

Research has found that the victims of bullying can experience long-lasting depression, anxiety, and sadness. There are many examples of victims of online bullying dropping out of school, needing psychological counseling, isolating themselves from friends and family, and, in the most extreme cases, committing suicide or other violent acts. Victims of online bullying are often bullied by friends and people they know.

In addition to the victim, often the family and friends of the victim of online bullying suffer from the abuse. It can be difficult to cope with the continued suffering and anguish of a child, friend, or student. Parents often blame themselves for being unable to help their children and often don't understand why their son or daughter is so harmed by online bullying. Some online bullying targets the family and friends of the victim.

10
Great Questions to Ask a Counselor

1. While playing an online game with other players, it's common to hear negative comments said about the other players. Is this considered online bullying?

2. What can I do if someone sends me repeated unwanted text messages?

3. What can I do if strangers start harassing me on my social network page?

4. What kinds of things should I share or not share about myself with people online?

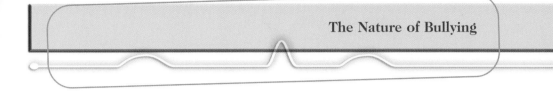

5. A couple of my friends have made a Web site just to make fun of another kid from school. They say some pretty nasty things, and it seems like it's getting out of control. What can I do to get them to stop?

6. My friend is being bullied by other kids in our school, and now it's starting to happen online. Who should I tell about this?

7. Another student who bullies me is now pretending that I was bullying her by telling a moderator at my favorite chat site. Now I am locked out of the Web site and there is nothing I can do about it. What should I do?

8. Is it all right to bully someone if they're already being picked on by other students?

9. Are there harsher punishments for bullies who pick on others because of their race, religion, or sexual orientation?

10. How do I deal with the feelings I have when I am bullied?

chapter two
Online Bullying and the Law

Bullying and cyber-bullying are treated very similarly in the eyes of the law. By definition, bullying and cyberbullying perpetrators and victims must be minors, under the age of eighteen. If the bully is over the age of eighteen, the aggressive actions are not considered bullying but harassment. Bullying is a juvenile crime and most often left to parents, guardians, and schools to deal with. Harassment is an adult crime and is usually dealt with by law enforcement. But now that bullying has gone online, it is very hard for parents to know when or if it happens and even harder to prevent it from happening again.

Cyberbullying is difficult to prove. The victim must show clear evidence of the bully's actions and must show clear evidence of the bully's identity. So unless the victim takes the time to record all the bullying behavior and can prove who the online attacker is, it is very difficult to get police involved. Unfortunately, many local police departments are neither well equipped nor trained to deal with cyberbullying.

Adding to the difficulty of prosecuting online bullying are the privacy protection laws that Internet and cell phone providers must abide by. In order for anyone to get access to the Internet activity logs of another person, he or she must usually get a court-ordered subpoena. Once you have the raw Web usage data, you may still need further subpoenas to get access to the

Bullies usually pick on people who appear weak. Showing confidence and pride is one way to thwart a bully.

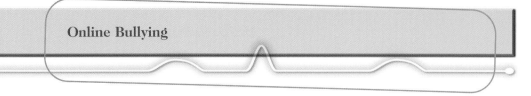

bully's activity on social networks, the servers of which may reside in a different state and be subject to a different set of laws.

Phoebe Prince

Phoebe Prince was the victim of widespread bullying by her classmates at South Hadley High School in South Hadley, Massachusetts. Prince was just fifteen when she committed suicide on January 14, 2010. She had been bullied by several of her classmates, and she was eventually so distraught by the bullying, taunting, and threatening that she took her own life.

Prince did all the right things to report the bullying: she told her friends, she told her teachers, and she told her parents. Prince's bullies were numerous and worked together to make her torment substantial. Nine students were indicted in relation to Prince's suicide for charges ranging from harassment and stalking to statutory rape. The cases are still pending at this time.

As a result of Prince's death and the death of another Massachusetts child, eleven-year-old Carl Joseph Walker-Hoover, lawmakers in Massachusetts chose to draft new legislation to address bullying. The new anti-bullying law was passed May 4, 2010, and it provides a framework and requirements for training and reporting in schools whenever bullying occurs. Schools are required to inform parents when a student is bullied and are required to provide training to faculty to facilitate appropriate response and support.

Cyberharassment and Cyberstalking

It is very important to note the differences between bullying, harassment, and stalking. Bullying, as mentioned earlier in this chapter, is between two minors, under the age of eighteen. Harassment and stalking, although similar to bullying, require that the perpetrator be at least eighteen years old. Harassment is defined almost identically. to bullying and involves repeated actions to cause disruption or discomfort on the part of the victim, and the

Even juvenile offenders can pay a hefty price for bullying.

perpetrator is an adult. Stalking involves following and an additional layer of intimidation in which the perpetrator makes threats of bodily harm or death to the victim.

This is important to know for several reasons. First, if you are the victim of bullying by an adult, that adult can face serious consequences from the law. Second, if you are still in high school and turn eighteen, it can be easy to forget that you are no longer considered a juvenile and that your online (or in-person) bullying can have very serious consequences for you.

Sexual Harassment and Bullying

Whenever sexuality is introduced to online bullying, the situation becomes much more serious and almost always brings additional layers of legal classification. Language that is used to hurt the feelings of another based on their sex or sexual orientation or which involves threats of sexual assault is very serious and has much more serious consequences than more typical bullying behavior.

There are many types of sexually based bullying. The most common is slander that is used to inflict pain and a feeling of inadequacy on the part of the victim. When a bully uses language that crosses the line from teasing or taunting to threatening or suggestive, the act of bullying moves from bullying to sexual harassment. Further, if the bullying is aimed at someone who may be LGBT, the aggression may be considered discriminatory and subject to certain state hate crime laws, which can carry very serious consequences.

Sexting is another serious problem because of the nature of sexual consent and statutory laws. Sexting between two minors can be considered a major offense because state law assumes that minors are not able to consent sexually. So sending a "sext" to someone may have serious consequences, even if the sender and the recipient both consented to the sexting. Additionally, sexts never really disappear. They can be erased from a phone but may exist on other phones or the phone company's server permanently.

Race and Religion and Bullying

Instances of bullying in which the victim is targeted because of his or her race or religion, or when the taunts used by the bully focus on the victim's race or religion, are treated seriously. Courts and schools have adopted more aggressive stances on racial and religious-based intimidation and will generally apply much more protection to victims and more punishment to bullies. Racial and religious bullying can also be considered a possible hate crime and possibly bring about serious legal consequences for the perpetrator.

chapter three

Identifying Online Bullying

One of the more difficult aspects of stopping cyberbullying is that many children and teens don't know that they have been victims. Too many children are exposed to harsh treatment online at an early age, making them less sensitive to harmful behavior. Most kids assume that people saying mean things about them is just natural and that it is something that everyone has to deal with online. Lack of awareness of bullying by the victim does not make the bullying all right, and it doesn't mean that the victim isn't suffering from it. Victims of bullying may assume that everyone online is mean to everyone else and because of this they may have inappropriate expectations of social settings and may develop social problems as a result.

Another challenge is that children and adolescents who are the targets of cyberbullying may be unwilling to speak out because of feelings of shame, embarrassment, humiliation, and pride, which can confuse the victims and make them feel like they shouldn't tell anyone about the bullying.

Signs of Online Bullying

The most likely people to spot online bullying are family, friends, and teachers. It is often hard to see changes in behavior, but there are some signs that you can look for: sleeping too much, not sleeping enough, avoiding social settings, avoiding friends, changes in mood, and changes in health. Any major behavioral change that seems substantially out of character for a young person may be a sign that he or she is going through some form of crisis and may be in need of intervention.

It is especially hard to determine if these changes or uncharacteristic behaviors are caused by something like online bullying or if they are normal adolescent or teen changes that can be very common. However, favoring caution and supportive intervention can make it possible to quickly discover if a young person has been subject to bullying or some other trauma.

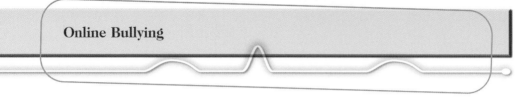

Ryan Halligan

Ryan Halligan was thirteen years old at the time of his suicide on October 7, 2003, and was the victim of a large-scale cyberbullying campaign by students from his school. Halligan was bullied mostly through AOL Instant Messenger (AIM). He was accused of being gay, had a girl pretend to like him only to gain information to give to his bullies, and was encouraged by others to kill himself.

Halligan's case is one of the earliest documented cases of suicide brought about by the effects of online bullying and is frequently cited in research for legislation about bullying and the role of schools. Halligan's father has become a staunch advocate for education about bullying and has traveled widely to talk to students and teachers about online bullying and its effects.

Other Methods of Online Bullying

Bullies tend to search for areas of weakness that provide the greatest impact on their victims. Physical differences are very easy to exploit by bullies. Calling someone fat, ugly, short, or other derogatory terms is a quick and easy way for a bully to cause a negative impact. Bullies will also go after things like race, religion, class, and nationality. Because the victim is not in the same room as the bully, it can feel much safer to bully online. Many people behave much differently online than they do in person.

In the case of online video game networks and multi-player games, bullies will do their best to sabotage the

Video games are meant to be fun. However, some bullies use their social networking capabilities to attack their victims online.

success of the victim in the game and the social environment. Many games involve interactions with other live players. Some games even allow players to speak with each other using headsets, creating many opportunities for both in-game and verbal bullying.

On social networks, bullies are given ample tools to victimize in front of a vast audience. Having a stage and a massive audience is very empowering for some bullies,

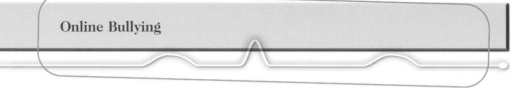

making the urge to bully much stronger. Bullies will post derogatory messages and sensitive images, create bully groups, and attempt to humiliate victims.

Until recently, cell phone bullying has been relegated to excessive texting and calling and verbal and text-based abuse. However, as cell phones become more sophisticated and provide more access to the Internet, they have become common vehicles for bullying and abuse.

Digital audio and video have become common on the Web, cell phones, and most Internet-connected devices. Many families have digital cameras and video recorders to capture their experiences. In a family setting or in a private setting, some young people will let down their guard in a way that they wouldn't ordinarily around their peers. Bullies have found that publishing those private videos on the Web is a very powerful way of harming their victims. The sheer volume of videos on sites like YouTube is so great that it is very easy for bullies to post videos that are hurtful.

Dealing with the Effects of Cyberbullying

Researchers have found that victims of online bullying can develop low self-esteem, depression, anxiety, and social disorders. In the worst cases, bullying can result in self-harm and suicide. The only people who are able to effectively and safely address the psychological and social problems of an individual are trained teachers, counselors, psychologists, psychiatrists, social workers, and parents.

Often the first people most likely to see online bullying are the close friends of the victim or the bully.

The friends may have conflicting emotions about what to do for their friend. Among many teens and adolescents, there is an unspoken understanding of group preservation through silence. Kids don't tell teachers or parents about bullying because their school or peer culture has enforced the faulty belief that silence is the best way to protect a friend. In fact, the truth is the exact opposite—telling teachers and parents about bullying is the best thing that a young person can do to protect a friend.

Talking to a counselor or mentor about bullying can be intimidating, but it is the best thing one can do to heal from the abuse.

For some victims, one of the most painful parts of online bullying is that they have no safe place to hide or retreat to escape their bullies. Adding to the situation is the fact that victims are often bullied by children from their school. The victim is bullied at school and online. The victim's entire life can feel like a constant state of being bullied, even in his or her own home.

Schools throughout the United States have very different standards for dealing with online bullying. Some states require that schools take mandatory action, but some states give schools no authority to act. The courts in the United States have often not supported the schools' right to intervene in cases where activity outside of school impacts the students' well-being. This has left victims of bullying, and their parents, on their own to deal with bullies.

Schools are adopting policies to address the new ways that children interact with each other via technology. Some schools have attempted to create rules that impact the non-school time of students in an effort to curb bullying with punitive actions like suspension and expulsion. However, in most cases, the courts have deferred to the rights of the parent to determine appropriate non-school time, curbing the effectiveness of anti-bullying measures at schools.

chapter four

How to Prevent Online Bullying

Victims of bullying often feel a very natural urge for revenge. Some feel it would be liberating and empowering to give back to the bully exactly what he or she gave: pain and suffering. Unfortunately, the most common consequence of retaliation is further bullying. It is very common for bullying to escalate quickly and grow from a small problem into a big one.

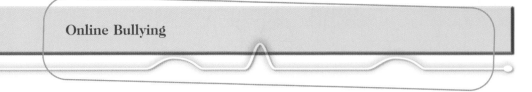

Often, the initial reaction of a victim will set the stage for all future bullying. The more a victim reacts, the more likely the bully will seek to target that person. In the case of online bullying, most victims who return similar taunts or language to a bully cause the problem to escalate.

In the worst cases, some bullies have used the retaliatory language of their victims to have the victim banned from a Web site or network. This is a very real possibility and happens more frequently than one might think.

Protecting Your Personal Information

Because the Internet is so large, it is very important to protect your personal information very carefully. It is crucial that everyone keep in mind the importance of doing so.

The Internet has become much bigger in the last ten years, and the number of online sites and services that we use on a daily basis has grown tremendously. The average teen probably uses a cell phone, Facebook, Twitter, and more on any given day to connect with friends and social groups. Although these sites and services are separate from each other, it is not difficult to follow a victim from one place to another and make bullying a constant theme of the victim's online experience.

To prevent this from occurring, it is important to use safe practices at all times. This is true for children and adults alike. Bullies are getting sophisticated, and clever bullies can figure out how to find their victims wherever they may go.

Tina Meier is the mother of Megan Meier, a thirteen-year-old girl who committed suicide after being bullied.

Speaking Up

Victims of bullying tend to deal with the problem by remaining silent and hoping it goes away. Some victims feel that it is their responsibility to deal with their bullies and that involving their parents is a sign of weakness. This is not true at all. Failing to deal with the negative feelings that come from bullying can lead to long-term mental health issues, including depression, anxiety, and potentially suicide.

It is very hard for some victims to tell anyone about their suffering. They often feel weak and embarrassed about the bullying and would rather suffer alone than admit the truth to anyone else. It is very important for victims to be made aware that reporting bullying to an adult is the right move in any situation. Reporting bullying will help both the victim and the bully.

Stopping the Cycle

Bullies take pleasure in making their targets look weak and afraid. Therefore, the best way for a victim to react to a bully is to be strong and react with courage. If bullies are using physical or verbal threats against you, the best way to deal with them is to tell them to stop or leave you alone and immediately leave the area where they are.

Victims can also become bullies themselves in the process of trying to defend themselves. Most often, the cause of the bully-victim effect is self-defensive behavior toward bullies that goes too far and becomes offensive behavior. The line between defense and offense is hard to see sometimes, and it is important for kids and teens to talk with their parents and teachers about where to draw this line.

It is very important that you never say anything mean or unkind when you are confronting a bully because doing so will only aggravate the bully and reinforce the behavior. Bullies often suffer from mental and emotional anguish as a result of other things. So when you say something that attacks the bully, he or she will gain more motivation to bully.

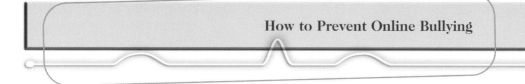

The most common form of online bullying is flaming in online chat sites and social networks. Flaming happens when someone says something to another with the goal of getting the other person upset and getting them to react. Flaming is an attack that is usually directed at total strangers, and it usually has the effect of provoking online shouting matches. The only way to safely and effectively deal with flaming is to record it and report it.

When defending themselves, victims may go too far and become bullies themselves. Researchers have found that in some cases, 27 percent of victims of online bullying become bullies themselves.

It is easy to escalate the bully's level of aggression when an outside party steps in. The "hero" who steps in needs to know that he or she needs to tell the bully to stop and separate the victim from the bully. If the hero attempts to teach the bully a lesson, that hero can become a bully.

chapter five

Documenting Online Bullying

Cyberbullying is happening in new ways and using new technologies faster than the law can keep up. Because of this, the burden of documenting cyberbully activity falls on the victim. Whenever bullying occurs, the first thing a victim should do is document the bullying activity. Documenting online events by taking screenshots, saving text messages, saving e-mail, making copies of images, and recording the URL

of Web sites are all important. Documentation is critical for proving that bullying occurs and proving who the bully is.

The kind of documentation needed to prove bullying activity depends on the nature of the bullying and the form of technology used by the bully. If the bullying is conducted through text messages, the victim should keep all the text messages. If the bullying is through cell phone calls, copies of phone bills should be kept to show who called you, along with the cell phone's call history log.

If the bullying is done via a Web site, screenshots should be taken and copies of the page source made. The page source code will contain some identifying information about who the Web site creator is. It is also possible to look up who owns the Web site by using online tools like Whois, which will tell you the publicly available information about a Web site owner.

Reporting Online Bullying

The first people a victim should report bullying to are parents or guardians; they are the ones who have the most immediate authority to intervene. Once parents have been informed, they will then be able to determine whether to involve school or the police.

Web site and social network site moderators should also be informed about bullying. Most Web sites with forums or chat rooms have community moderators who watch the dialogue and behavior on those sites. Moderators have the ability investigate the behavior on their Web sites to stop aggressive behavior. They can also

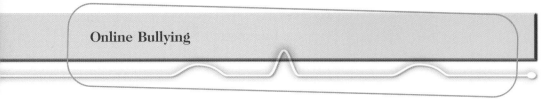

ban users from Web sites if the behavior is severe and the bullies refuse to stop.

Web sites like Facebook have many moderators and safety personnel who work around the clock to try to keep the Web site safe and friendly. If you are bullied on Facebook, you should immediately contact Facebook to report the incident so that personnel can research, document, and report the bullying to authorities.

Healthy Online and Offline Practices

Parents need to be involved with the online lives of their children in order to understand the new social dynamics of adolescent and teenage life and to be able to spot any signs of trouble that may arise. In addition, parents need to create stronger ties to their children's schools and the parents of other students. Parents should share information with each other in order to better understand the networks of communication that their children use. Parents also have the ability to share information about bullying and any changes that they see in their children and their peers.

Very often, the last parties ever involved in cases of bullying, unless compelled by law, are Web sites, social networks, communications providers, and other enterprises. There are some social networks, like Facebook, which spend time and money to police their Web sites to make sure that children are protected from bullying and other online threats.

Quite often, the first reaction the parent of an online bullying victim has is to restrict the online access of that

victim. Although this is an attempt to protect the child, restricting access to online social networks can have a very negative effect on the child. Young people today grew up with social networks and have formed very concrete relationships and aspects of their identity through them. Depriving a victim of his or her healthy online relationships during a time of crisis can cause added pain and suffering for the child.

Healthy offline interpersonal activities are very important to the social and psychological well-being of children of all ages. In times of crisis, it is important to reinforce positive self-esteem and positive interpersonal relationships. Parents and schools need to foster options for kids suffering through bullying so that they have constructive outlets and activities. Getting kids and teens involved in after-school groups and extracurricular activities is a great way to supplant their online social networks with real-world ones.

MYTHS AND FACTS

Myth: Online bullying is not as harmful as other types of harassment.

Fact: Online bullying is just as, if not more, harmful than other types of bullying. Unlike face-to-face harassment, messages sent over the Web can stay in cyberspace forever and haunt the victim for years.

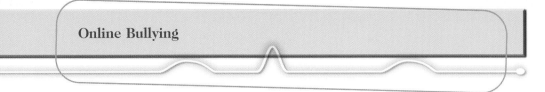

Myth: I'm bullied at school, so I should stay offline to avoid being attacked on the Web.

Fact: While staying offline completely could protect you from online bullying, it's not necessarily a healthy solution to the problem, just a way of avoiding it. You should be able to enjoy online socializing like everyone else.

Myth: I'll never get caught bullying someone online. The Internet is so big, they'll never find me.

Fact: While it is possible to be anonymous online, it is very easy to determine where messages originate on the Web, right down to the geographical position of a cell phone. Modern computer and Web forensics can retrieve very detailed information about the origin of online messages. You can find out who sent a message, where the message physically originated on the Internet, what kind of computer was used to send the message, and much more.

anxiety A psychological or physiological condition that can cause a sense of fear, uneasiness, or dread. Many victims of bullying experience anxiety before, during, or after they are bullied. Anxiety is a serious condition and should be treated by a doctor or psychologist.

computer forensics Computer forensics is the science of gathering evidence of computer crimes. Forensic specialists use sophisticated tools to uncover evidence even when people have tried to erase their hard drive, hide their online identity, use anonymous Web servers, and more.

cyberharrassment The use of disturbing, threatening, or intimidating behavior online for the sake of disrupting or upsetting the victim. Cyberharrassment is very similar to cyberbullying except that the perpetrator or victim is old enough to be considered an adult.

cyberstalking Obsessive and repetitive behavior that includes threats of violence or bodily harm to victim. Stalking behavior is often predatory and the perpetrator will do anything in order to gain access to the victim on whichever online Web sites or services the victim uses.

depression Depression is a psychological or physiological condition causing sadness, lethargy, anxiety, or fear. Many victims of bullying can develop depression. It is a serious mental and medical condition and should be treated by a doctor or psychologist.

intervention An intervention is a protective measure that family, friends, teachers, or counselors use to help bring about a safe and healthy outcome for a person in crisis. In the context of online bullying an intervention can be staged for a bully or a victim in order to help them realize that the situation they face is serious and that they have support and help all around them.

online moderator Anyone who is employed by a Web site or who is officially authorized by the site to monitor the behavior of site users. Typically moderators look for violations to the Terms of Service of the Web site, which are usually different for each site.

relational bullying Bullying intended to harm the social situation and standing of another individual. This bullying method is indirect, meaning that the bully does not directly attack the victim using physical or verbal methods, rather the bully uses status and social networks to hurt the victim's social status.

sexting Sending text messages or SMS messages with language and pictures of a sexual nature. Although sexting is completely legal between consenting adults, it is illegal if the participant is not of legal consenting age.

text war A text war involves one or more people sending large volumes of text messages to another individual. The effect of the text war is to flood the victims text message box and to cause the victim the financial burden of having to pay for all of the text messages.

verbal bullying Verbal attacks used to create a disruptive or harmful outcome. Verbal bullying can be name-calling, using harsh words, or other language.

American Academy of Child and Adolescent Psychology (AACAP)
3615 Wisconsin Avenue NW
Washington, DC 20016-3007
(202) 966-7300
Web site: http://www.aacap.org
The AACAP is the leading national professional medical association dedicated to treating and improving the quality of life for children, adolescents, and families affected by mental, behavioral, or developmental disorders.

A Thin Line
1515 Broadway, 45th Floor
New York, NY 10036
(212) 846-3723
Web site: http://www.athinline.org
MTV's A Thin Line campaign was developed to empower young people to identify, respond to, and stop the spread of digital abuse. The campaign is built on the understanding that there's a "thin line" between what may begin as a harmless joke and something that could end up having a serious impact on you or someone else.

BullyingCanada.ca
376 Westmorland Street, Unit 107
Fredericton, NB E3B 3M5
Canada
(877) 352-4497 ext. 203

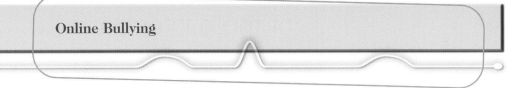

Web site: http://www.bullyingcanada.ca

BullyingCanada.ca is a youth-created Web site dedicated
     to educating and preventing bullying. It has volun-
     teers who provide crisis intervention, by phone and
     e-mail, for anyone in need.

Cyberbullying Research Center
5353 Parkside Drive
Jupiter, FL 33458-2906
(561) 799-8227
Web site: http://www.cyberbullying.us

The Cyberbullying Research Center is dedicated to pro-
     viding up-to-date information about the nature,
     extent, causes, and consequences of cyberbullying
     among adolescents.

i-SAFE, Inc.
6189 El Camino Real, Suite #201
Carlsbad, CA 92009
(760) 603-7911
Web site: http://www.isafe.org

Founded in 1998, i-SAFE, Inc. is the leader in Internet
     safety education.

National Association of School Psychologists
4340 East West Highway, Suite 402
Bethesda, MD 20814
(301) 657-0270
Web site: http://www.nasdonline.org

The National Association of School Psychologists (NASP)
     is the premier source of knowledge, professional

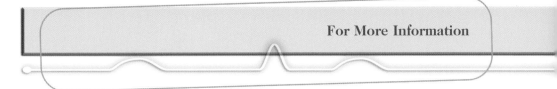

development, and resources for empowering school psychologists to ensure that all children attain optimal learning and mental health.

National Crime Prevention Council
2001 Jefferson Davis Highway, Suite 901
Arlington, VA 22202
(202) 466-6272
Web site: http://www.ncpc.org/cyberbullying
The National Crime Prevention Council's mission is to be the nation's leader in helping people keep themselves, their families, and their communities safe from crime.

Stop Bullying Now
5600 Fishers Lane
Rockville, MD 20857
Web site: http://www.stopbullyingnow.hrsa.gov
Stop Bullying Now is a project of the Health Resources and Services Administration (HRSA), an agency of the U.S. Department of Health and Human Services. It is the primary federal agency for improving access to health care services for people who are uninsured, isolated, or medically vulnerable.

StopCyberbullying.org
185 Hillcrest Avenue
Wyckof, NJ 07481
(201) 463-8663
Web site: http://www.stopcyberbullying.org
StopCyberbullying.org is dedicated to educating students, teachers and parents about how to spot cyberbullying

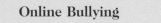

and how to effectively deal with both the victim and the bully.

Wired Safety
185 Hillcrest Avenue
Wyckof, NJ 07481
(201) 463-8663
Web site: http://www.wiredsafety.com
Wired Safety is among the leading experts in Internet and
digital safety, privacy and security, wired, wireless
and mobile, in the world. Comprised of thousands of
unpaid volunteers from all walks of life, experts from
the Wired Safety Group can respond to media
inquiries about actual cases and cybercrime and
abuse victims, Internet sexual predators, cyber security, Internet privacy, and all aspects of cyberlaw.

Web Sites

Due to the changing nature of Internet links, Rosen
Publishing has developed an online list of Web sites
related to the subject of this book. This site is updated
regularly. Please use this link to access the list:

http://www.rosenlinks.com/tmh/bull

Agatston, Patricia W., Robin M. Kowalski, and Susan P. Limber. *Cyber Bullying: Bullying in the Digital Age.* Malden, MA: Blackwell Publishing, 2008.

Barbour, Scott. *School Violence.* Framington Hills, MI: Greenhaven Press, 2006.

Bauman, Sheri. *Cyberbullying: What Counselors Need to Know.* Alexandria, VA: American Counseling Association, 2011.

Breguet, Teri. *Frequently Asked Questions About Cyberbullying* (FAQ: Teen Life). New York, NY: Rosen Publishing, 2007.

Carroll, Jamuna. *America's Youth.* Framington Hills, MI: Greenhaven Press, 2008.

Churchill, Andrew H., and Shaheen Shariff. *Truths and Myths of Cyber-Bullying* (New Literacies and Digital Epistemologies). New York, NY: Peter Lang, 2010.

Coloroso, Barbara. *The Bully, the Bullied, and the Bystander: From Preschool to High School—How Parents and Teachers Can Help Break the Cycle.* New York, NY: Harper Resources, 2009.

Friedman, Lauri S. *Cyberbullying* (Introducing Issues with Opposing Viewpoints). New York, NY: Greenhaven Press. 2011.

Hinduja, Sameer, and Justin Patchin. *Bullying Beyond the Schoolyard: Preventing and Responding to Cyberbullying.* Thousand Oaks, CA: Corwin Press, 2008.

Hinduja, Sameer, and Justin Patchin. *Cyberbullying Prevention and Response: Expert Perspectives.* New York, NY: Routledge. 2011.

Jacobs, Thomas A. *Teen Cyberbullying Investigated: Where Do Your Rights End and Consequences Begin?* Minneapolis, MN: Free Spirit Publishing, 2010.

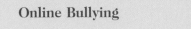

MacEachern, Robyn, and Geraldine Charette. *Cyberbullying: Deal with it and Ctrl Alt Delete It* (Deal With It). Halifax, Nova Scotia, Canada: Lorimer, 2011.

McQuade, Samuel C. III, James P. Colt, and Nancy Meyer. *Cyber Bullying: Protecting Kids and Adults from Online Bullies*. Westport, CT: Praeger Publishing, 2009.

Raum, Elizabeth. *Tough Topics: Bullying*. Chicago, IL: Heinemann Library, 2008.

Rogers, Vanessa. *Cyberbullying: Activities to Help Children and Teens to Stay Safe in a Texting, Twittering, Social Networking World*. London, England: Jessica Kingsley Publishers, 2010.

Shariff, Shaheen. *Confronting Cyber-Bullying: What Schools Need to Know to Control Misconduct and Avoid Legal Consequences*. New York, NY: Cambridge University Press, 2010.

Shariff, Shaheen. *Cyber-Bullying: Issues and Solutions for the School, the Classroom and the Home*. New York, NY: Routlege, 2008.

Willard, Nancy E. *Cyberbullying and Cyberthreats: Responding to the Challenge of Online Social Aggression, Threats, and Distress*. Champaign, IL: Research Press, 2007.

Willard, Nancy E. *Cyber-Safe Kids, Cyber-Savvy Teens: Helping Young People Learn to Use the Internet Safely and Responsibly*. San Francisco, CA: Jossey-Bass, 2007.

Winkler, Kathleen. "Bullying, How to Deal with Taunting, Teasing and Tormenting." *Issues in Focus Today*. Berkeley Heights, NJ: Enslow Publishers, 2005.

A
anti-bullying measures, 18, 28

B
bully-victims, 4, 5, 32, 33

C
Clementi, Tyler, 8–10
cyberstalking, 19–20

D
depression, 14, 26, 31

E
e-mail, 6, 34

F
Facebook, 11, 30, 36
flaming, 33

H
Halligan, Ryan, 24
happy slapping, 12
hate crimes, 20, 21

L
LGBT youth, 9–10, 20

O
online bullying
    documenting, 34–37
    identifying, 22–28

law and, 16–21, 28, 34, 36
myths and facts, 37–38
nature of, 4–15
preventing, 29–33
questions to ask, 14–15

P
polling, 6
Prince, Phoebe, 18

R
relational bullying, 5, 7, 8

S
self-esteem, 5, 26, 37
sexting, 6, 12, 21
social networks, 11, 14, 18, 25,
    30, 33, 35, 36, 37
suicide, 8, 9, 10, 14, 18, 24,
    26, 31

T
text wars, 11–12
Twitter, 30

V
verbal bullying, 5, 7–8, 25,
    26, 32
video posting, 6, 9, 10, 12, 26

W
Walker-Hoover, Carl, 18
Whois, 35

About the Author

Peter Ryan is an IT consultant with many years of experience in social networking and online communities. He has managed large social Web sites for children, where he first saw the effects of online bullying. Ryan has dedicated his career to helping people use technology efficiently and safely. He lives in Saratoga Springs, New York, with his wife, Aubrey, and two dogs.

Photo Credits

Editor: Nick Croce; Photo Researcher: Marty Levick